Phonics Friends

Alex in the Box Shop
The Sound of X

The Child's World

By Cecilia Minden and Joanne Meier

box

fox

six

Published in the United States of America
by The Child's World®
PO Box 326
Chanhassen, MN 55317-0326
800-599-READ
www.childsworld.com

A special thank you to Scott Johnson and his family for participating in the production of this book and to the staff of the UPS store for their patience and understanding.

The Child's World®: Mary Berendes, Publishing Director

Editorial Directions, Inc.: E. Russell Primm, Editorial Director and Project Editor; Katie Marsico, Associate Editor; Judith Shiffer, Associate Editor and School Media Specialist; Linda S. Koutris, Photo Researcher and Selector

The Design Lab: Kathleen Petelinsek, Design and Page Production

Photographs ©: Photo setting and photography by Romie and Alice Flanagan/Flanagan Publishing Services: cover, 4, 6, 8, 10, 14; Getty Images/Photodisc Blue: 16, 18; Getty Images/Taxi/Stephen Simpson: 12; Getty Images/Stone/TSI Pictures: 20.

Library of Congress Cataloging-in-Publication Data
Minden, Cecilia.
   Alex in the box shop : the sound of X / by Cecilia Minden and Joanne Meier.
      p. cm. — (Phonics friends)
   Summary: Simple text featuring the sound of the letter "x" describes how Alex helps his Uncle Max in his box shop.
   ISBN 1-59296-309-9 (library bound : alk. paper)
   [1. English language—Phonetics. 2. Reading.] I. Meier, Joanne D. II. Title. III. Series.
   PZ7.M6539Al 2004
   [E]—dc22
                                            2004003544

Note to parents and educators:

The Child's World® has created Phonics Friends with the goal of exposing children to engaging stories and pictures that assist in phonics development. The books in the series will help children learn the relationships between the letters of written language and the individual sounds of spoken language. This contact helps children learn to use these relationships to read and write words.

The books in this series follow a similar format. An introductory page, to be read by an adult, introduces the child to the phonics feature, or sound, that will be highlighted in the book. Read this page to the child, stressing the phonic feature. Help the student learn how to form the sound with her mouth. The Phonics Friends story and engaging photographs follow the introduction. At the end of the story, word lists categorize the feature words into their phonic element. Additional information on using these lists is on The Child's World® Web site listed at the top of this page.

Each book in this series has been carefully written to meet specific readability requirements. Close attention has been paid to elements such as word count, sentence length, and vocabulary. Readability formulas measure the ease with which the text can be read and understood. Each Phonics Friends book has been analyzed using the Spache readability formula. For more information on this formula, as well as the levels for each of the books in this series please visit The Child's World® Web site.

Reading research suggests that systematic phonics instruction can greatly improve students' word recognition, spelling, and comprehension skills. The Phonics Friends series assists in the teaching of phonics by providing students with important opportunities to apply their knowledge of phonics as they read words, sentences, and text.

This is the letter *x.*

In this book, you will read words that have the *x* sound as in:

excited, box, fox, and six.

Alex is excited.

He is in Uncle Max's shop.

Uncle Max sells boxes.

Alex puts the boxes in piles.

Little boxes go in one pile.

Big boxes go in another pile.

People come in to buy boxes.

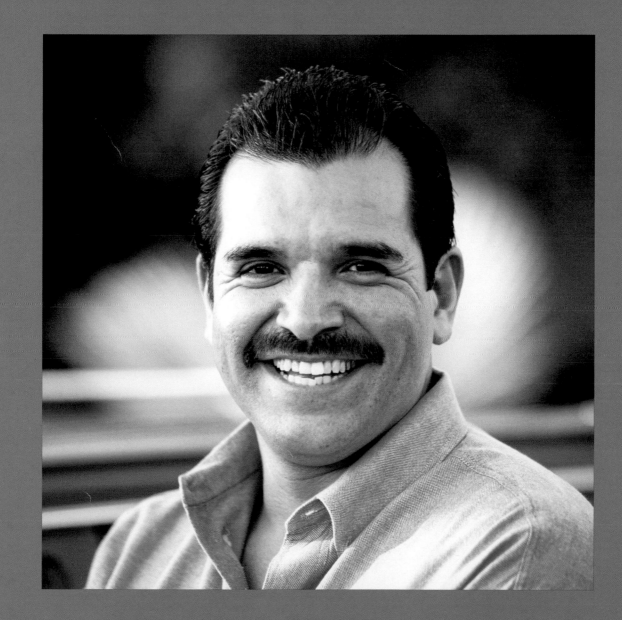

Mr. Cox comes into the shop.

He needs a box for a toy fox.

The fox is for his son Rex.

Rex has the chicken pox.

Mrs. Baxter comes in next.

She needs a big box for Roxy.

Roxy is Mrs. Baxter's cat.

Why does Roxy need a big box?

Roxy just had six kittens!

Fun Facts

Chicken pox is a disease that spreads easily. You can get chicken pox at any age, but patients are usually between two and six years old. Once you are exposed to chicken pox, it takes about two weeks for the red, itchy bumps to appear. You may run a fever. If you've had chicken pox once, you probably won't catch it again. A shot from your doctor may help you avoid catching chicken pox.

A male fox is known as a dog. A female fox is called a vixen, and a baby fox is called a kit. Foxes are found on every continent except Antarctica. There are more than 25 different types of foxes. Some foxes can live to be 14 years old.

Activity

Building a Box Village

Gather boxes of different shapes and sizes to create your village. Begin with the largest boxes on the bottom and add the medium-sized boxes next. The smallest boxes should be on the top. You can tape or glue them together as you build. If you want your village to be colorful, cover your boxes with construction paper before you begin. Make sure to add windows and doors to your buildings!

To Learn More

Books
About the Sound of X
Flanagan, Alice K. *A Fox: The Sound of X*. Chanhassen, Minn.: The Child's World, 2000.

About Boxes
Fleming, Candace, and Stacey Dressen McQueen (illustrator). *Boxes for Katje*. New York: Farrar, Straus and Giroux, 2003.
Morrison, Toni, Slade Morrison, and Giselle Potter (illustrator). *The Big Box*. New York: Hyperion Books for Children, 1999.

About Chicken Pox
Dealey, Erin, and Hanako Wakiyama (illustrator). *Goldie Locks Has Chicken Pox*. New York: Atheneum Books for Young Readers, 2002.
Maccarone, Grace, and Besty Lewin (illustrator). *Itchy, Itchy Chicken Pox*. New York: Scholastic, 1992.

About Foxes
Carle, Eric. *Hello, Red Fox*. New York: Simon & Schuster Books for Young Readers, 1998.
Geisel, Theodor (Dr. Seuss). *Fox in Socks*. New York: Beginner Books, 1965.
Marshall, James. *Fox on the Job*. New York: Dial Books for Young Readers, 1988.

Web Sites
Visit our home page for lots of links about the Sound of X:
http://www.childsworld.com/links.html

Note to Parents, Teachers, and Librarians: We routinely check our Web links to make sure they're safe, active sites—so encourage your readers to check them out!

X Feature Words

Proper Names

Alex

Baxter

Cox

Max

Rex

Roxy

Feature Words in Final Position

box

fox

pox

six

Feature Words in Medial Position

excited

next

About the Authors

Cecilia Minden, PhD, directs the Language and Literacy Program at the Harvard Graduate School of Education. She is a reading specialist with classroom and administrative experience in grades K–12. She earned her PhD in reading education from the University of Virginia. Cecilia and her husband Dave Cupp enjoy sharing their love of reading with their granddaughter Chelsea.

Joanne Meier, PhD, has worked as an elementary school teacher and university professor. She earned her BA in early childhood education from the University of South Carolina, and her MEd and PhD in education from the University of Virginia. She currently works as a literacy consultant for schools and private organizations. Joanne Meier lives with her husband Eric, and spends most of her time chasing her two daughters, Kella and Erin, and her two cats, Sam and Gilly, in Charlottesville, Virginia.

PEACHTREE